A PERSONAL NOTE

I've decided to make this coloring book for my children, so they can spend time not only coloring letters, animals, flags and other symbols, but also learning about different countries and cultures.

I've chosen 50 countries for this book. If you like watching soccer, feel free to give this book to your little one while watching FIFA World Cup 2022, because you will learn many interesting things about all participating countries in this World Cup and other countries too.

These countries are organized by alphabetic order. Two full pages devoted to each country with some extra space to take notes or draw something.

I've done my best to choose the most known symbols, icons, landmarks, national food and drinks, dances, famous people and places, national flowers or animals shown in the pictures for each country.

Explore the World with this Smart Coloring book learning about countries, capitals, flags, continents, national languages, population, quotes, proverbs, symbols and much more!

Educational, fun and made with love for children and adults.

ARGENTINA

Buenos Aires

Continent: South America
Country: Argentina
Capital: Buenos Aires
Official language: Spanish
Currency: Argentine peso
Population: 46,149,299 (2022)

Quote / Saying
Dress the monkey in silk and it is still a monkey.

Let's learn!
'Hi' in Spanish is 'Hola'

AUSTRALIA

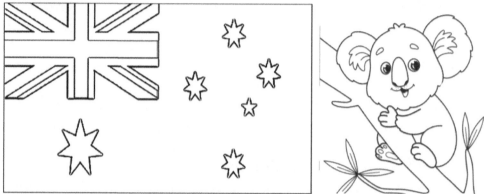

Canberra

Continent: Australia / Oceania
Country: Australia
Capital: Canberra
National language: English
Currency: Australian dollar
Population: 25.69 million (2020)

Quote / Saying
A bird in the hand is worth two in the bush.

BELGIUM

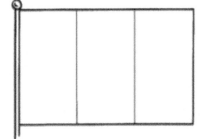

Brussels

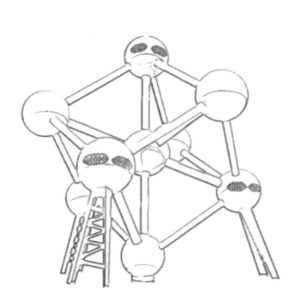

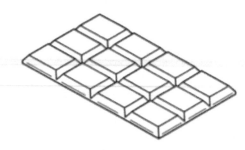

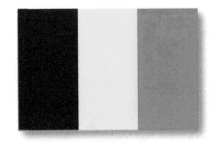

Continent: Europe
Country: Belgium
Capital: Brussels
Official languages:
Dutch, French,
German
Currency: Euro
Population: 11.56 million (2020)

Quote / Saying
The bee, from her industry in the summer, eats honey all the winter.

BRAZIL

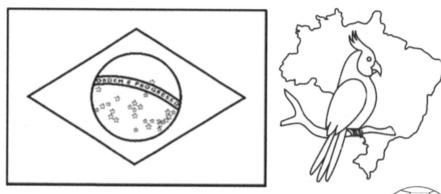

Brasília

Continent: South America
Country: Brazil
Capital: Brasilia
Official languages:
Portuguese
Currency: Brazilian real
Population: 212.6 million (2020)

Quote / Saying
Remember to always smile.
(Roberto Carlos)

CAMEROON

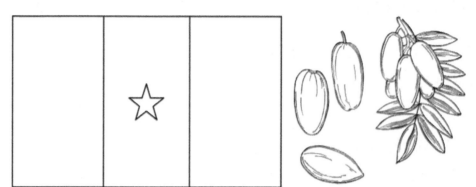

Yaoundé

Continent: Africa
Country: Cameroon
Capital: Yaoundé
Official languages: French, English
Currency: Central African CFA franc
Population: 26.55 million (2020)

Quote / Saying
A building of sand falls as you build it.

CANADA

Ottawa

Continent: North America
Country: Canada
Capital: Ottawa
Official languages: English, French
Currency: Canadian dollar
Population: 38.01 million (2020)

Quote / Saying
You miss 100% of the shots you don't take.
(Wayne Gretzky)

CHILE

Santiago

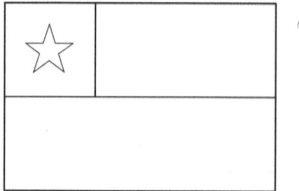

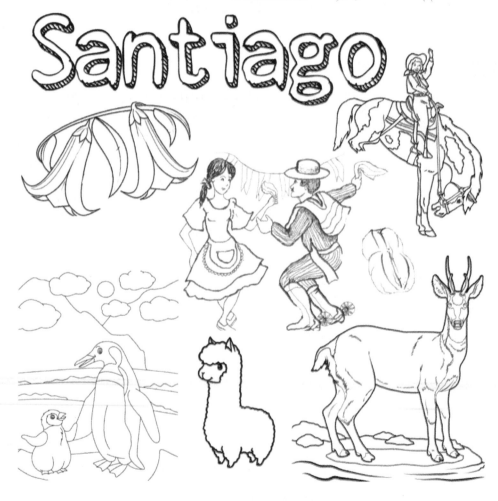

Continent: South America
Country: Chile
Capital: Santiago
Official language: Spanish
Currency: Chilean peso
Population: 19.12 million (2020)

Quote / Saying

Life is tough - and you have to be tougher than life to change the world.
(Sebastian Pinera)

CHINA

Beijing

Continent: Asia
Country: China
Capital: Beijing
Official language: Mandarin
Currency: Renminbi
Population: 1.402 billion (2020)

Chinese proverb
Better to light a candle than to curse the darkness.

COLOMBIA

Bogotá

Continent: South America
Country: Colombia
Capital: Bogota
Official language: Spanish
Currency: Colombian peso
Population: 50.88 million (2020)

Colombian proverb

Dios le da pan al que no tiene dientes.

"God gives bread to those who have no teeth," is a very Colombian way of remarking that a person has something they cannot, or will not, appreciate.

COSTA RICA

San José

Continent: North America (Central America)
Country: Costa Rica
Capital: San Jose
Official language: Spanish
Currency: Costa Rican colón
Population: 5.094 million (2020)

Costa Rican phrase
Pura Vida.
"Pure Life", but it can be used as "great", "fantastic", "hello", "nice to meet you", "thank you", or "you're welcome"

CROATIA

Zagreb

Continent: Europe
Country: Croatia
Capital: Zagreb
Official language: Croatian
Currency: Croatian Kuna
Population: 4,047,949 (2022)

Popular sayings

Jabuka ne pada daleko od stabla.
English equivalent:
The apple does not fall far from the tree.

DENMARK

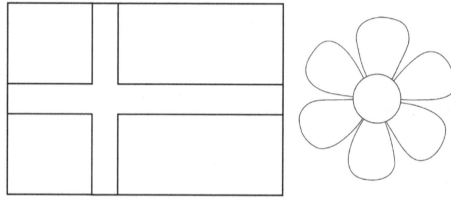

Copenhagen

Continent: Europe
Country: Denmark
Capital: Copenhagen
Official language: Danish
Currency: Danish Krone
Population: 5,839,084 (2022)

Quote

The most important thing is to try to do your best.
(Christian Erikson)

ECUADOR

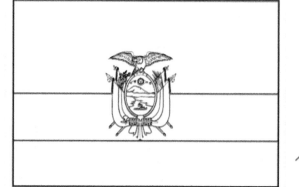

Quito

GUENCA

Continent: South America
Country: Ecuador
Capital: Quito
Official language: Spanish
Currency: United States Dollar
Population: 17.64 million (2020)

Quote

Anyone who is afraid to lose isn't ready to win.
(Fabrizio Moreira)

Let's learn!

'Thank you' in Spanish is 'Gracias'

EGYPT

Cairo

Continent: Africa & Asia
Country: Egypt
Capital: Cairo
Official language: Arabic
Currency: Egyptian pound
Population: 102.3 million (2020)

Quote

You can tell whether a man is clever by his answers.
You can tell a man is wise by his questions.
(Naguib Mahfouz)

ENGLAND

London

Continent: Europe
Country: England
Capital: London
National language: English
Currency: Pound sterling
Population: 55.98 million (2018)

Quote

Nothing is impossible, the word itself says 'I'm possible'!
(Audrey Hepburn)

ETHIOPIA

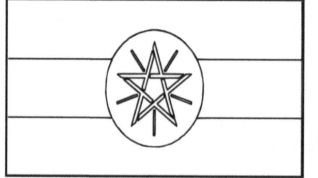

Addis Ababa

Continent: Africa
Country: Ethiopia
Capital: Addis Ababa
Official languages:
Amharic, Somali, Oromo,
Tigrigna, Afar
Currency: Ethiopian birr
Population: 115 million (2020)

Quote
Helping others isn't a chore; it is one of the greatest
gifts there is.
(Liya Kebede)

FRANCE

Paris

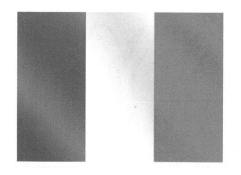

Continent: Europe
Country: France
Capital: Paris
National language:
French
Currency: Euro, CFP frank
Population: 67.39 million (2020)

Quote

Kind words do not cost much. Yet they accomplish much.
(Blaise Pascal)

Let's learn!

'Hello' in French is 'Bonjour'.

GERMANY

Berlin

BENZ

Continent: Europe
Country: Germany
Capital: Berlin
National language: German
Currency: Euro
Population: 83.24 million (2020)

Quote
Once something is a passion, the motivation is there. (Michael Schumacher)

Let's learn!
'Thank you' in German is 'Danke'.

GHANA

Accra

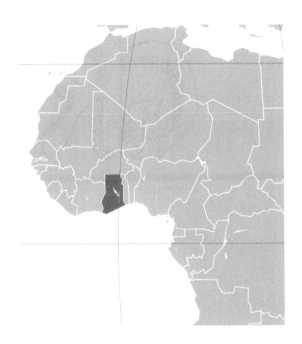

Continent: Africa
Country: Ghana
Capital: Accra
Official language: English
Currency: Ghanaian cedi
Population: 31.07 million (2020)

Quote
Knowledge is power. Information is liberating. Education is the premise of progress, in every society, in every family.
(Kofi Annan)

GREECE

Athens

Continent: Europe
Country: Greece
Capital: Athens
National language: Greek
Currency: Euro
Population: 10.72 million (2020)

Quote

It's not what happens to you, but how you react to it that matters.

(Epictetus)

ICELAND

Reykjavík

Continent: Europe
Country: Iceland
Capital: Reykjavík
National language:
Icelandic
Currency: Icelandic króna
Population: 366,425 (2020)

Quote
Health is never going to go out of fashion.
(Magnus Scheving)

INDIA

New Delhi

Continent: Asia
Country: India
Capital: New Delhi
Official languages:
Hindi, English
Currency: Indian rupee
Population: 1.38 billion (2020)

Quote
Self-belief and hard work will always earn you success.
(Virat Kohli)

IRAN

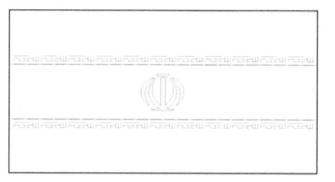

Tehran

Continent: Asia
Country: Iran
Capital: Tehran
Official language: Persian
Currency: Iranian rial
Population: 83.99 million (2020)

Quote
Have patience. All things are difficult before they become easy.
(Saadi)

ITALY

Rome

 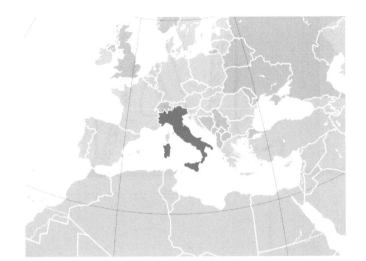

Continent: Europe
Country: Italy
Capital: Rome
Official language: Italian
Currency: Euro
Population: 59.55 million (2020)

Quote
We do not remember days, we remember moments.
(Cesare Pavese)

JAPAN

Tokyo

Continent: Asia
Country: Japan
Capital: Tokyo
National language: Japanese
Currency: Japanese yen
Population: 125.8 million (2020)

Quote
Failure is the key to success; each mistake teaches us something.
(Morihei Ueshiba)

KAZAKHSTAN

Astana

Continent: Europe & Asia
Country: Kazakhstan
Capital: Astana
Official languages:
Kazakh, Russian
Currency: Tenge
Population: 18.75 million (2020)

Quote

Knowing another's language and culture makes a person equal to those people.
(Abai Kunanbaev)

MEXICO

Mexico City

Continent: North America
Subregion: Central America
Country: Mexico
Capital: Mexico City
Official language: Spanish
Currency: Mexican peso
Population: 128.9 million (2020)

Quote

Clay can be dirt in the wrong hands, but clay can be art in the right hands.
(Lupita Nyong'o)

Let's learn!

'How are you doing?' in Spanish is '¿Qué tal?'

MONGOLIA

Ulaanbaatar

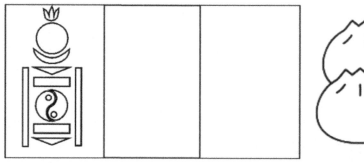

Continent: Asia
Country: Mongolia
Capital: Ulaanbaatar
Official language: Mongolian
Currency: Mongolian tögrög
Population: 3.278 million (2020)

Mongolian proverb

While horse is strong travel to see places.

MOROCCO

Rabat

Continent: Africa
Country: Morocco
Capital: Rabat
Official languages: Arabic, Amazigh
Currency: Moroccan dirham
Population: 36.91 million (2020)

Moroccan proverb
If you are responsible of a problem, you should find the solution.

NETHERLANDS

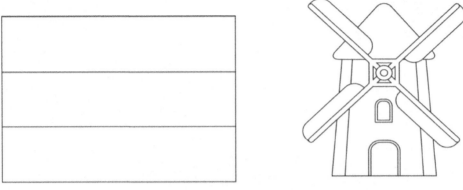

Amsterdam

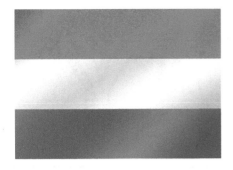

Continent: Europe
Country: The Netherlands
Capital: Amsterdam
Official language: Dutch
Currency: Euro
Population: 17.44 million (2020)

Quote

Great things are done by a series of small things brought together.
(Vincent Van Gogh)

NORWAY

Oslo

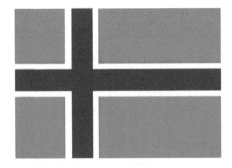

Continent: Europe
Country: Norway
Capital: Oslo
Official languages:
Norwegian, Sami
Currency: Norwegian krone
Population: 5.379 million (2020)

Quote

It is better to go skiing and think of God, than go to church and think of sport.
(Fridtjof Nansen)

PAKISTAN

Islamabad

Continent: Asia
Country: Pakistan
Capital: Islamabad
Official languages: Urdu, English
Currency: Pakistani rupee
Population: 220.9 million (2020)

Quote

To be the best, I had to work harder than everyone else.

(Jahangir Khan)

PANAMA

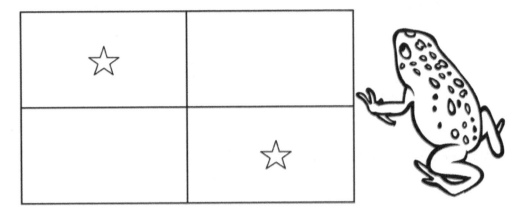

Panama City

Continent: North America
Subregion: Central America
Country: Panama
Capital: Panama City
Official language: Spanish
Currency: United States Dollar, Panamanian balboa
Population: 4.315 million (2020)

Quote
Because I have a little bit more, that means I'm better than you? No. Unacceptable.
(Mariano Rivera)

Let's learn!
'Very good' in Spanish is 'Muy bien'.

PERU

Lima

Continent: South America
Country: Peru
Capital: Lima
Official language: Spanish
Co-Official languages: Quechua,
Aymara, other indigenous languages
Currency: Sol
Population: 32.97 million (2020)

Peruvian proverb
It is better to prevent than to cure.

Let's learn!
'Thank you so much' in Spanish is 'Muchas gracias'

POLAND

Warsaw

Continent: Europe
Country: Poland
Capital: Warsaw
Official language: Polish
Currency: Polish zloty
Population: 37.95 million (2020)

Quote
The future starts today, not tomorrow.
(Pope John Paul II)

PORTUGAL

Lisbon

Continent: Europe
Country: Portugal
Capital: Lisbon
Official language: Portuguese
Currency: Euro
Population: 10.31 million (2020)

Portuguese proverb

Saco vazio não para em pé

Literal Translation: An empty bag doesn't stand upright.

This is a saying a kid will hear if they stay outside playing all day without coming in to eat. It's a pretty literal expression: if you don't eat, you'll feel sick and may even pass out. A bag with nothing in it just flies away.

PUERTO RICO

San Juan

Continent: North America
Free Associated State:
Puerto Rico
Capital: San Juan
Official language: Spanish, English
Currency: United States Dollar
Population: 3.194 million (2020)

Quote

Music has the power to inspire the world.
(Bad Bunny)

QATAR

Doha

Continent: Asia
Country: Qatar
Capital: Doha
Official language: Arabic
Common language: English
Currency: Qatari riyal
Population: 2.931 million (2021)

Proverb
One day is for you and another is against you.

SAUDI ARABIA

Riyadh

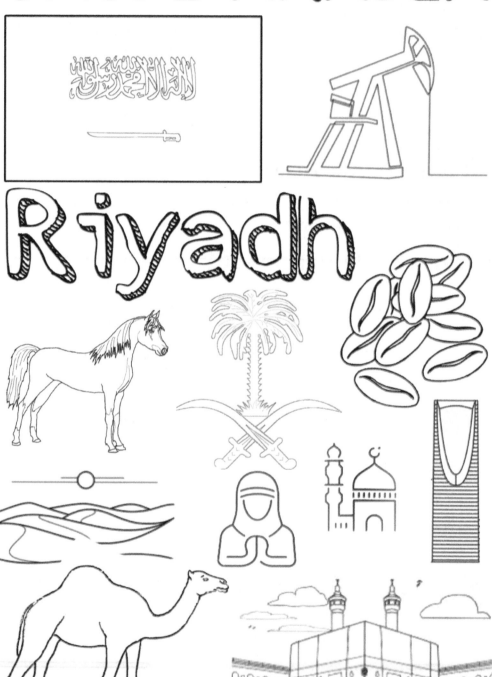

Continent: Asia
Country: Saudi Arabia
Capital: Riyadh
Official language: Arabic
Currency: Saudi riyal
Population: 35.34 million (2021)

Quote

Where there are difficulties, there will always be opportunities.

(Mohamed Bin Issa Al Jaber)

SENEGAL

Dakar

Continent: Africa
Country: Senegal
Capital: Dakar
Official language: French
Currency: West African CFA franc
Population: 17.2 million (2021)

Quote

You have to believe in yourself and believe in what you are doing all the time.

(Sadio Mane)

SERBIA

Belgrade

Continent: Europe
Country: Serbia
Capital: Belgrade
Official language: Serbian
Currency: Serbian dinar
Population: 6.844 million (2021)

Quote

To build a friendship takes so much time and so many years. To ruin it, just seconds.

(Vlade Divac)

SOUTH KOREA

Seoul

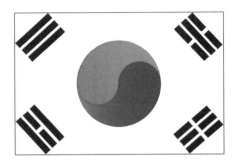

Continent: Asia
Country: South Korea
Capital: Seoul
Official languages: Korean, Korean Sign Language
Currency: South Korean won
Population: 51.74 million (2021)

Quote

Drink lots of water and get enough sleep. Try not to stress. Positive thoughts only!
(Dahyun)

SPAIN

Madrid

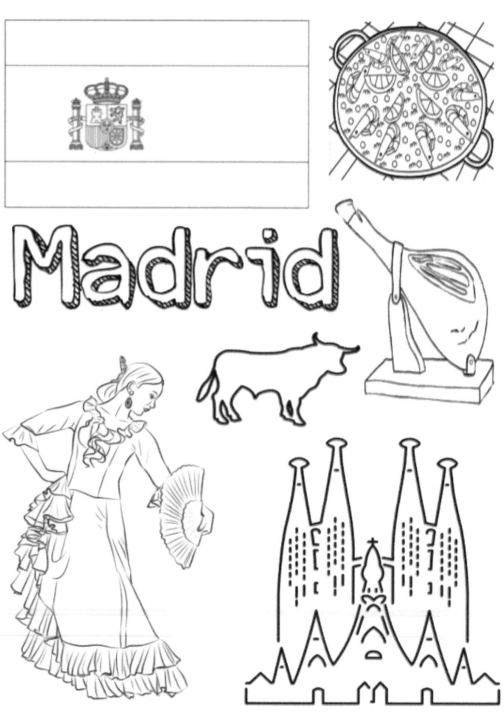

Continent: Europe
Country: Spain
Capital: Madrid
Official language: Spanish
Currency: Euro
Population: 47.33 million (2021)

Quote
Action is the foundational key to all success.
(Pablo Picasso)

SWITZERLAND

Bern

Continent: Europe
Country: Switzerland
Capital: Bern
Official languages:
 French, German, Italian,
Romansh
Currency: Swiss franc
Population: 8.698 million (2021)

Quote
When you look at billionaires, many of them share
one characteristic: They were not born billionaires.
(Sergio Ermotti)

TUNISIA

Tunis

Continent: Africa
Country: Tunisia
Capital: Tunis
Official language: Arabic
Spoken languages:
Tunisian Arabic, Berber, French,
Italian, English
Currency: Tunisian dinar
Population: 11.94 million (2021)

Quote
A human being is not a machine. Especially when it comes to creating.
(Azzedine Alaia)

TURKEY

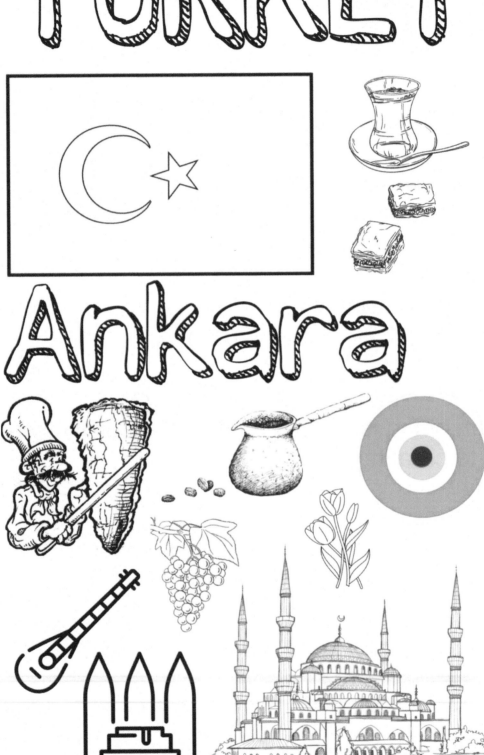

Ankara

Continent: Europe, Asia
Country: Turkey
Capital: Ankara
Official language: Turkish
Currency: Turkish lira
Population: 86,433,198 (2022)

Quote

Success is about persistence. You can only afford to be persistent in something you deeply enjoy.
(Cenk Uygur)

UKRAINE

Kyiv

Continent: Europe
Country: Ukraine
Capital: Kyiv
Official language: Ukrainian
Currency: Ukrainian hryvnia
Population: 43.81 million (2021)

Quote

The one who punches doesn't win. The one who dodges punches wins.

(Vitali Klitschko)

URUGUAY

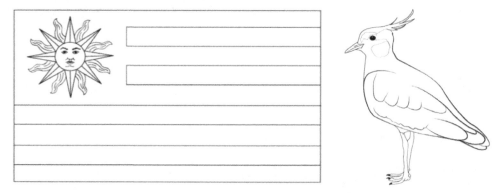

Montevideo

Continent: South America
Country: Uruguay
Capital: Montevideo
Official languages: Spanish, Uruguayan Sign Language
Currency: Uruguayan peso
Population: 3.485 million (2021)

Quote

We always try to correct what we did wrong; you can always learn something when you lose.
(Diego Godin)

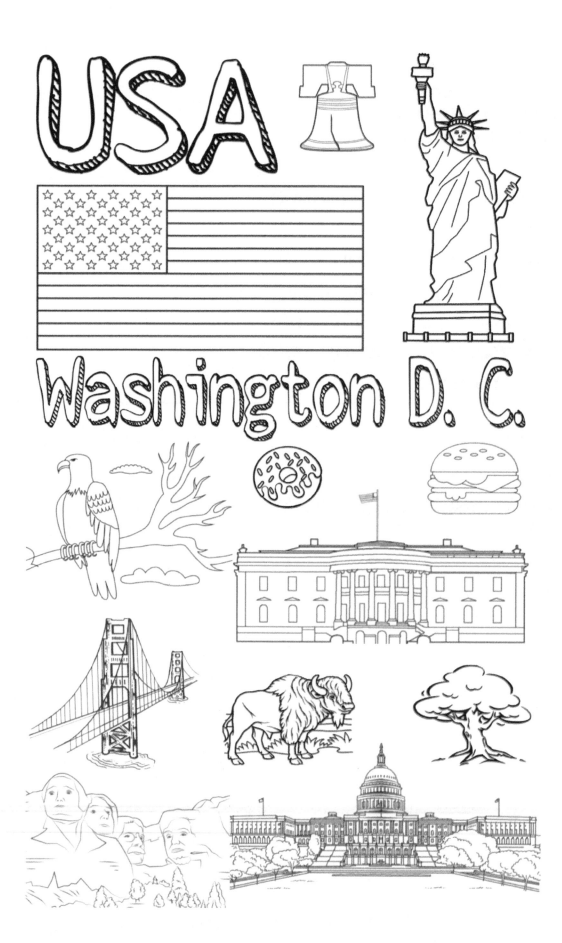

Continent: North America
Country: The United
States of America
Capital: Washington D.C.
National language:
English
Currency: U.S. dollar
Population: 331.9 million (2021)

Quote
Believe you can and you're halfway there.
(Theodore Roosevelt)

WALES

Cardiff

Continent: Europe
Country: Wales
Capital: Cardiff
Official languages:
Welsh, English
Currency: Pound sterling
Population: 3.136 million (2019)

Quote

Make new friends, but keep the old; Those are
silver, these are gold.
(Joseph Parry)

Made in the USA
Las Vegas, NV
21 April 2023

70922367R00057